PLUNGE

orca sports

PLUNGE

ERIC HOWLING

ORCA BOOK PUBLISHERS

Library and Archives Canada Cataloguing in Publication

Howling, Eric, 1956-,
Plunge / Eric Howling.
(Orca sports)

Issued in print and electronic formats.
ISBN 978-1-4598-1419-6 (softcover).—ISBN 978-1-4598-1420-2 (pdf).—
ISBN 978-1-4598-1421-9 (epub)

I. Title. II. Series: Orca sports
PS8615.O9485P58 2017   jC813'.6   C2017-900778-5   C2017-900779-3

First published in the United States, 2017
Library of Congress Control Number: 2017932500

Summary: In this high-interest sports novel for teens,
Cade has to use his triathlon training to save his family.

*Orca Book Publishers is dedicated to preserving the environment and has printed
this book on Forest Stewardship Council® certified paper.*

Orca Book Publishers gratefully acknowledges the support for its publishing
programs provided by the following agencies: the Government of Canada
through the Canada Book Fund and the Canada Council for the Arts,
and the Province of British Columbia through the BC Arts Council
and the Book Publishing Tax Credit.

Cover photography by iStock.com
Author photo by Theo Wilting

ORCA BOOK PUBLISHERS
www.orcabook.com

Printed and bound in Canada.

20 19 18 17 • 4 3 2 1

To my sons.

Chapter One

Chapter One

This race was going to be different.

This time Cade would leap from the starting block and cut through the water ahead of every other swimmer. Including Gavin Groves. Especially Gavin Groves.

Cade was tired of swimming in Gavin's wake. Always coming in fourth, or fifth, or even worse. He wanted to stand on the podium. Just once. That's all he was asking for. All he wanted. And this was the race to do it. Trials to select Team Alberta for the Canada Summer Games started today. The top three of each event would make the team. The rest would be out of luck.

Cade had trained just as hard as Gavin or any other fourteen-year-old on the Blue Sharks swim club. Being jolted awake by his alarm every weekday morning before dawn. Stumbling from his warm bed. Wolfing down a bowl of oatmeal at the kitchen table. Jumping on his mountain bike and pedaling to the pool as the sun came up. It had been his routine for the entire summer.

The 200-meter I.M. (Individual Medley) was the toughest event, but it was his best. The race not only tested swimmers' ability in all four individual strokes but also their endurance. Four laps of the 50-meter pool. Cade wasn't the best at any single stroke, but he was pretty decent at all four. This race was his chance to prove himself against Gavin and all the other swimmers of his age in the province.

"Take your marks."

Each of the eight swimmers stood on his starting block and crouched into start position. Cade was in lane two. Gavin was two lanes over. Cade put one foot ahead of the other, gripped the front edge of the block with his fingers and got ready to spring into action. There wasn't a ripple in the pool. There wasn't a sound from the crowd. There wasn't a muscle that moved.

The electronic horn beeped.

All of Cade's frozen energy exploded as the sound of the electronic pulse shot through his body. His coiled leg muscles released, launching him high into the air over the water. His arms reached out like Superman before piercing the smooth blue surface below. In seconds the water was whipped into a white froth like a milkshake in a blender. Eight boys churned through the pool, arms whirling, legs kicking.

Through his goggles Cade focused on the narrow lane ahead of him. He never once looked left or right. He'd worry where

Gavin and the rest of the competitors were later. The first length was butterfly, the most tiring stroke of all. His arms extended out to the sides like wings, then swung forward together, propelling his upper body out of the water. Beneath the surface his legs dolphin-kicked, driving him forward.

He felt the water rush by and could see the end of the pool getting closer with every stroke. He reached out and touched the wall, then pushed off onto his back. Feeling good. All his early-morning practice was paying off.

Cade shot through the water like a torpedo. With his face now out of the water, it was easier to sneak a peek across the lane ropes at the other swimmers. Their brightly colored swim caps were easy to spot. He saw a red one and a green one ahead of him. No sign of Gavin and his Shark cap. He was rocking this race! If he could hold on, he'd finish third.

Cade dug down deep. His shoulders turned, whirling his arms over his head one at a time. With each stroke he pulled his cupped hands back alongside his body. Left...right...left...right. He knifed through the water.

He touched the wall and arched to do the backflip "suicide turn" he'd practiced a million times. Pushing off the wall onto his front, he glided as far as he could underwater before surfacing to start the breaststroke. He could see the other swimmers ahead of him. A blue cap had joined the red and the green. Gavin had moved into third place! *Not for long*, Cade thought. There was still a chance he could catch Gavin on the last lap. Third place was still within reach.

Cade touched the wall with both hands, took a deep breath, swiveled and pushed off. This last length of freestyle was the fastest leg of the race. Every swimmer would be giving his all to finish strong.

Cade knew he could catch Gavin and the lead swimmers, but he'd have to pull out all the stops. Forget breathing every three strokes—who had time to breathe in the most important race of his life?

He took a quick breath only when his oxygen-deprived body screamed at him.

He picked up his stroke count, thrashing his arms through the water even faster. With his head down, he couldn't see where the other swimmers were. But he couldn't worry about the competition. All he could do was swim flat out and hope to pass them.

His lungs really started to burn. His arms began to ache. His legs could barely kick anymore, but he had to push forward. Just half a lap more.

Cade thought about how sweet it would be to stand on the podium. How swimmers from all over the province would clap their hands and look at him with new respect. How Coach Pedersen would smile and say he'd known Cade could do it all along. How Gavin would finally have to admit Cade was the better swimmer. They'd all know soon enough what Cade Dixon was made of.

This was it. Just a few more meters. He took one last gulp of air, then forced his arms to pull with every last ounce of energy. Three meters...two meters...one meter...reach...touch!

Cade grabbed the wall and lifted his head. Heart still pounding, he looked to his right. He didn't expect to see anyone. He truly thought Gavin and the others were still racing for second. But Gavin was already at the wall, grinning.

"Thought you had me, Dixon."

And he wasn't alone. Red cap and green cap had finished too. *Am I seeing this right?* He pulled up his goggles and shot a glance to his left. *Yep.* All the other competitors were in, trying to catch their breath. Some were even high-fiving each other. Cade couldn't believe it.

He had finished dead last.

Chapter Two

"You'll do better next time."

Jasmine Wong skipped over to where Cade was toweling off. "Jazz" was Cade's friend and one of the top swimmers on the Blue Sharks. Her black hair was cut short so it would fit easily under her cap. She wasn't as tall as some of the other girls, but her strength more than made up for it. She had powerful arms and shoulders built up from years of grueling practices.

Her legs were strong too. Her flutter kick was famous at the club.

"I'm not so sure there'll be a next time," Cade said. "I gave it my best shot, but I still sucked."

"You just had an off day," Jazz said, smiling as usual. "You'll be on the podium soon."

Jazz was the only one to talk to him right after the race. Gavin was too busy pounding fists with the guys who had come first and second. They were pumped knowing they had qualified for Team Alberta. Not that Cade wanted to hear what Gavin had to say anyway.

"Cade, you got slayed," Gavin said, waving his arm around like a sword.

Cade narrowed his eyes. He was jealous but knew Gavin had earned his spot on the team fair and square. He hadn't.

"Summer Games, here I come," Gavin called over his shoulder as he walked toward the medal ceremony. "I'll send you a postcard from Winnipeg."

An ache started to grow in Cade's gut. The familiar pain that came from thinking he wasn't good enough. He turned back to his only friend. "How was your race?"

"Okay," Jazz said, shrugging her shoulders.

Cade knew what that meant. *Okay* was code for "kicking butt." It didn't matter what race Jazz entered, she usually came first. Jazz was an awesome swimmer.

Coach Pedersen walked along the edge of the pool to where Cade and Jazz were standing. He had the broad shoulders of an Olympic swimmer. Cade had often seen him doing lengths in the pool by himself after practice. It had been years since Coach had swum competitively, but he looked like he still could. He was the real deal.

"Good effort, Cade. You were right up there with the other guys until the last lap."

"Yeah, I guess I just ran out of gas."

"A little more practice and you'll catch Gavin."

Cade gritted his teeth. "I guess you're right, Coach."

But Cade wasn't sure Coach was right. He didn't know if all the practice in the world would make him as fast as Gavin was now. Cade was a good swimmer, but he was just a little too short and too slow to be a great swimmer.

At least Cade had the 200-meter free-style relay to look forward to. Coach usually picked him to be one of the four swimmers for the Blue Sharks team. He wasn't the lead swimmer, but it still felt good to be on the squad.

"Coach, the relay is coming up this afternoon," Cade said.

"Sure is, and I've entered a strong team."

"What time should I be ready?"

Coach looked down at his shoes. "Uh, you can take it easy for the rest of the day."

"What do you mean?"

"I had to make a tough call," Coach said, frowning. "I've chosen Gavin to be our fourth guy."

"What? He doesn't usually swim the relay."

"I know, but you just didn't seem to have it in you today. And he did."

Jazz jumped in front of Coach. "It was just one race," she pleaded. "He'll be better this afternoon."

Coach shook his head and crossed his arms. "I've made my decision. It wasn't easy. But these are the finals, and the winners go to the Canada Summer Games. We need the best team possible. I just don't think it's your day, Cade. I'm sorry." Coach put his hand on Cade's shoulder briefly, then turned and made his way back to the coaches' table.

Cade couldn't believe it. He hadn't thought things could get any worse after the last race, but they had. Now there was no reason to hang around. At every other swim meet, he would have stayed until the end to cheer on his teammates. But what was the point now?

"Let's bounce," Cade said to Jazz.

"You know I can't," she replied. "I'm swimming the girls' 200-meter relay in an hour."

"Whatever," Cade said. "I'm getting out of here. Stay and swim your stupid race."

Cade stomped into the men's change room. The metal door of his locker clanged as he threw it open. He pulled on his shorts and T-shirt, shoved his towel and swim gear into his backpack and headed for the door. He didn't need this place.

Outside the aquatic center he strapped on his helmet, unlocked his mountain bike from the rack and hopped on. He sped down the path, not caring what direction he went. All he wanted to do was get away from the pool. Most days he'd take it easy, letting his arm and leg muscles unwind after a long practice. He'd ride slowly along the Bow River, watching the ducks paddle along the surface.

Not today. He blasted his bike up and down the hills of the paved path. He zigzagged between joggers and walkers, almost knocking a couple of them down.

"Slow down!" an older woman called.

"You're going to kill someone!" a man shouted, shaking his fist.

If he wasn't such a good rider, he would have hit them for sure. But he wasn't going to slow down for anybody.

His bike's wheels were spinning as fast as his thoughts. *I want to be good at something. I have to be good at something. Trent is a star football player, always getting his name in the newspaper. Dad loves that. Can't shut up about that. If I can't make it to the Summer Games, what good am I?*

A couple more minutes and he'd be home. He geared up and stomped down hard on the pedals. His wheels tore around the final corner. He gripped the handlebars and put his head down for one final push. His eyes focused on the pavement zipping by below.

"Watch out!"

Cade looked up. But it was too late. A bike was speeding right toward him. The rider swerved to avoid the collision, going off the path but managing to stay on his bike. Cade wasn't so lucky. He had turned his front wheel so sharply that he lost control.

Plunge

He flew headfirst over his handlebars and crashed onto the pavement. He had been going so fast, he didn't come to a stop until his body had skidded along the blacktop. He felt the skin ripping off his arms and legs. Blood oozed from his elbows and knees like ketchup from a bottle.

Chapter Three

Cade was still sprawled on the ground when the man approached him, wheeling his bike. He didn't look angry. Cade would have been if a kid had just run him off the path.

"You okay?" the man asked.

"I think so," Cade said, checking his bloodied arms and legs. This was definitely going to be his worst case of road rash ever.

"You might need a doctor to take a look at those cuts," the man said, leaning over to take a closer look. "They look fairly nasty."

The man was pretty old. About the same age as Cade's grandfather. He had gray hair that stuck out from his helmet. His face was tanned and crinkled behind a pair of dark sunglasses. He was wearing a special red biking shirt and sleek black bike shorts. On his feet were silver shoes that clicked on the pavement when he walked. He may have looked like an old weathered prune, but Cade thought he still looked pretty cool.

"Sorry about the crash," Cade said. "Totally my fault."

"Accidents happen," the man replied. He laid his bike down and then picked up Cade's to move it to the side of the path. "I remember wiping out in a big race back in 2009."

"What happened?" Cade asked, crawling to sit on the grass.

"I was hitting sixty kilometers an hour, screaming down a monster hill, when I got cut off by another bike. I hit the brakes—which turned out to be a big mistake."

Cade's eyes widened. Why was an old guy like this blasting down a hill at the same speed as a car? "Why? What happened?"

"My bike stopped, but I kept right on going. I took a terrible spill. I think there was more skin left on the road than there was on my legs," he said, laughing.

"I know the feeling," Cade said, holding up his arm to check his skinned elbow. "Too bad you had to quit the race."

"Quit? Are you kidding? You don't quit Ironman unless they put you on a stretcher and an ambulance takes you away. A medic slapped a couple of bandages on me, and I got back up on my bike. Came third in my age group. Not bad for a sixty-year-old."

Cade looked again at his arms and legs. After hearing the man's story, his injuries didn't seem so bad.

"Is Ironman a big bike race?" he asked.

"You've never heard of Ironman? It's more than a bike race. It's a big triathlon—the biggest."

Cade knew there were three sports in a triathlon but wasn't exactly sure which three. "What else do you do besides bike?"

"Every triathlon starts with a swim," the man said, sitting down beside him. "I'm George Grimsby, by the way," he said, holding out his hand.

"Cade Dixon. Nice to meet you."

"The second sport is biking." Mr. Grimsby stared at Cade's scratched-up bike and smiled. "I know you can ride fast, but you might want to work on your steering."

Cade took a closer look at the man's bike. It wasn't like any he had ever seen. Even just lying there it looked fast. It was thin and appeared to be made of some kind of special plastic. The handlebars were pointed straight ahead, not to the side like his. Cade noticed two big bottles filled with a bright-orange liquid attached to the tube under the seat. The pedals were different too.

The bike looked so space-aged, Cade wondered where it had come from. The future maybe.

Mr. Grimsby noticed Cade eyeing his bike and nodded. "Yup, she's a beauty."

"Is it heavy?" Cade asked. His mountain bike weighed a ton.

"See for yourself."

Cade winced as he stood. He didn't even know if he had enough strength to lift the bike. But it wasn't a problem. "I can't believe how light it is! I can hold it with one finger!"

"The frame is made with super-strong carbon fiber," Mr. Grimsby said, grinning. "The same stuff they use to make hockey sticks, tennis racquets, even fighter jets."

Cade put the bike down, still shaking his head in disbelief. "What's the third sport?"

"Running. By the time you finish the swimming and biking, you're sucking wind pretty bad. But you still have to lace up your shoes and give everything you've got."

"So it's swim, bike, run?"

"Yup, all three." Mr. Grimsby tilted his head. "What do you think? Could you see yourself ever doing a triathlon?"

Cade wasn't sure. But given the way things had gone down at the pool that morning, he was feeling like maybe his days of only swimming were over. Maybe switching it up wouldn't be so bad.

"What have I got to lose?"

Chapter Four

Cade heard the car doors slam in the garage. Seconds later his dad and brother came charging into the kitchen. It was early Saturday afternoon, and he had just sat down to eat the PB&J sandwich his mom had made him for lunch.

"What a game!" his dad said, slapping Trent on the shoulder pads. "Our boy was amazing."

Trent was the quarterback for the Calgary Broncos football team. He was still dressed in his uniform—orange jersey and white pants, just like the NFL Denver Broncos. Trent's team played in the Alberta Junior Football League against squads from Lethbridge, Red Deer and Edmonton.

Cade glanced at his brother. He was a mess. Grass stains smeared on the elbows and knees of his uniform. The back of his jersey ripped where a defensive lineman must have grabbed it. Dried blood on his passing arm.

Trent was two years older than Cade. He was a lot bigger and a lot stronger too. He outweighed Cade by twenty pounds and stood at least four inches taller. Standing there in his big shoulder pads Trent looked like a giant. Cade felt smaller in every way.

"Last play of the game, and Trent throws a perfect strike to our wide receiver in the end zone!" The words came flying out of his dad's mouth faster than a quarterback calling out signals at the line of scrimmage. "We won by a single point. Trent was the hero and got mobbed by his teammates!"

"Sounds like quite a game," his mom said. "But why don't you let Trent tell us about it? I think he was there too."

"You're right, Trent doesn't need me to tell you he's the star of the team and has a real chance to go pro one day. Tell 'em, Trent."

Cade waited for Trent to continue the story. He could have described every play of the fourth quarter. How he single-handedly rallied the team. How he threw the pass to score the winning touchdown. How the fans in the stands chanted his name. But he didn't. "It was no big deal," Trent said. "It was just a football game."

Cade knew his brother really was a star. He heard all the talk at school. How Trent was the best player on the Broncos. How he had an arm like a rifle. How he could run like a speedy halfback. When Cade sat in the cafeteria, girls would pass by him saying, "That's Trent's little brother!" Cade appreciated that Trent didn't brag about football all the time. Unlike his dad. His dad couldn't stop.

"*Just* a football game?" his dad said, getting red in the face. "Football is the greatest game there is! That's the way I was brought up. It's a real man's sport. Guys are getting hit every play. You've got to be tough to go hard for sixty minutes."

"Swimming is a sport too," Cade said. He was sick of hearing nothing but football talk.

"Barely," his dad replied. "There's no running. No tackling. No hitting the hard turf. You just dive in the water and swim for a couple of laps. No big deal, if you ask me."

Cade glared at his dad. He knew where this was going. He bit his lip to stop himself from saying something he'd regret later.

"When you and Trent were young, we gave you a choice, remember?" his dad said. "Play football or take swimming lessons. You took the easy way."

"You think swimming is so easy?" Cade snapped. It was hard not to fight back. "Then how come you can't do it?"

"I'm too old to learn how to swim." His dad's voice started to rise. "Besides, swimming is for little kids."

Trent turned to face his dad. "That's not true. Look at the Olympics. You think Michael Phelps is a little kid? He's six-five and ripped."

"Yeah, well, Cade is no Olympic star," his dad said, shaking his head. "I don't see any gold medals around his neck."

Trent stepped beside his brother. "Actually, I wish I *had* taken more lessons. I wish I could swim as well as Cade."

"I wouldn't worry about it, Trent," his dad said, calming down a bit. "It's not like you're ever going to need it. Especially when you're a pro football player."

His father was always favoring Trent's sport. Always cheering him on. Always going to his games. When was the last time he'd come to one of Cade's swim meets? Two years ago, that's when. Cade didn't win any ribbons that day either. His father never went back. It was like he didn't care unless Cade won. Now it was only his mom who sometimes came to the meets. And even she was coming less and less as he got older.

"Your father doesn't mean it," she said gently. "We're all proud of your swimming. You just had a bad day yesterday. There'll be better swim meets ahead."

"Cade got pretty scraped up too," Trent said, pointing at Cade's elbows and knees. The scabs were starting to look like strips of crispy bacon.

Cade's father glanced at the red scratches on Cade's arm and shook his head. "Those aren't real injuries. All Cade did was run into some old man and fall off his bike. It's not like he was tackled by a giant lineman while throwing a touchdown pass."

With only a single bite taken out of his sandwich, Cade stood up and pushed his plate across the table.

His dad narrowed his eyes. "What's the matter, you not hungry?"

Cade met his father's gaze, then quickly looked away. "Guess I lost my appetite."

Chapter Five

Cade rolled over in bed and yawned.

It was nine o'clock on a Monday morning and the first time he had slept in for months. Normally, he'd be at the pool doing lengths by now. But he wasn't sure he was going back to swimming. At least, not anytime soon. He was embarrassed to show his face. He couldn't beat Gavin or any of the other swimmers at the club. Coach Pedersen had always said to just do his best. But now he knew his best wasn't good enough. Or at least not good enough to be picked for the relay team. So why keep trying?

He stared up at the ceiling. He didn't know why his dad thought football was so much better than swimming, but he did. Cade had always hoped that if he won a swimming race, his dad might respect him more. Not pick on him so much. Maybe even think he was as good as Trent. But that dream was fading fast.

He got up and shuffled to the window. From his upstairs bedroom he could see all the houses that lined the street. He watched the sprinklers spraying back and forth, trying to keep the lawns green. He liked the hot days of August. It meant summer wasn't over and school was still a few weeks away. Now that he wasn't swimming all the time, the days were passing a lot more slowly.

Cade let out a sigh. He was about to turn away from the window when he spotted a man jogging down the sidewalk. It was Mr. Grimsby. A cap kept the bright sun out of his eyes, and a couple of small water bottles were attached to a belt around his waist.

Cade thought he must be training for his next triathlon. Wondering how far he was going, Cade threw on a T-shirt and pair of shorts and ran downstairs. He pulled on the basketball shoes he'd kicked off in the front hall the night before and raced out the door.

Not wanting to bother Mr. Grimsby, he didn't get too close. He kept back by about a block, being careful not to lose sight of him.

It wasn't long before Cade started to breathe hard. If he didn't slow down, he'd have to stop. He took smaller steps. At least now he didn't sound like a panting dog. He hoped he could hold that pace and follow Mr. Grimsby as far as he was going. But where *was* he going?

Mr. Grimsby ran past the elementary school, the playground with the swings, and three more blocks of houses in the neighborhood. Then he took a right turn and headed down a wooded trail toward

Fish Creek, a huge provincial park. This was getting into serious distance.

The path that followed the creek was one of Cade's favorite places to bike. He'd see people jogging and wonder why they looked so tired. Now he started to understand why. Trying to keep up with Mr. Grimsby was exhausting. Not only was Cade back to breathing hard, but his feet were starting to hurt. Maybe basketball kicks weren't the best choice for running long distance.

Up ahead Mr. Grimsby was reaching for one of his water bottles. *Good*, thought Cade. *Finally he'll stop to take a drink*. But Mr. Grimsby didn't stop. He grabbed his water bottle, took a sip and kept right on going.

Cade didn't think he could follow much farther. He had no water. Sweat was pouring down his face. His legs felt like rubber. And his feet were killing him. After a few more strides he stopped in the middle of the path and watched Mr. Grimsby disappear around a bend into the trees. Just like the pink

Energizer bunny on the TV commercials, he kept going and going.

What had made him think he could ever train for a triathlon? He couldn't even do the running part. He couldn't even keep up with an old man. How was he going to bike and swim as well? He turned around and headed home.

An hour later Cade was on the front steps of his house, sipping a tall glass of lemonade. He figured Mr. Grimsby would be at home having a cold drink as well. But down the street Cade noticed a man with gray hair coming toward him. It was Mr. Grimsby, and he was still jogging!

"How did your run go?" Mr. Grimsby asked, slowing to a walk in front of Cade's house.

"How did you know I was running?"

"I knew you were behind me, but I wanted to keep my pace."

"Are you training for a race?" Cade asked.

"You bet. There's a small triathlon in two weeks."

"Is it far away?"

"Nope, it's right here in Calgary. You should enter it."

"Me?"

"You can swim, bike and run, right?"

"Yeah, but..."

"So what's stopping you?"

Cade worried that his dad would think triathlon was another sissy sport. He was tired of getting put down all the time. Entering a triathlon would just give his dad another reason to pick on him.

"I'm not sure my dad would like it. And besides, I don't think I'm in good enough shape."

"Up to you, but I think you might enjoy yourself," Mr. Grimsby said. "If you change your mind, you know where to find me. I'll be out here every morning at nine o'clock sharp."

Chapter Six

Cade rode up to the bike rack outside the aquatic center. But he wasn't going to the pool today. He didn't want to risk running into Gavin or Coach Pedersen. He'd wait for Jazz to come out after practice.

A few minutes later Jazz pushed her way through the doors.

"Hey, buddy, what's up?" she said as she made her way to the bike rack.

"Wanted to say sorry for the other day."

"I know you didn't mean it," she said.

"Your race wasn't stupid. But I sure was for saying it."

"No biggie," she said with a shrug. "So where have you been? Everybody on the team misses you."

"You're just saying that," Cade said, rolling his eyes.

The pool doors swung open again, and Gavin marched out. "Well, if it isn't Cade the Fade."

"Very funny."

"Yup, the memory of you being a Blue Shark is just fading away."

"Zip it, Gavin," Jazz said. "You know Coach said he can come back anytime."

"Yeah, anytime he wants to get beat again," Gavin said, laughing as he walked away. "Adios, loser. I've got to go pack my bags."

Cade turned back to Jazz. "I don't know if I'm coming back."

"Maybe you just need to take some time off until after the Games."

"When are you leaving?" Cade asked.

"We fly to Winnipeg tomorrow. We'll be gone for a week."

"You're going to rock your events," Cade said. "Nobody can touch you in the 100 free."

"I have won most of my races this year," Jazz said matter-of-factly. "It would be nice to bring home a medal."

Cade nodded. "I bet it feels good to win."

"You don't have to come first to feel like you've won," Jazz said, punching him lightly on the shoulder. "Every time you swim a PB, you know you're getting faster. That's a win."

"Personal bests are great, "Cade said, "but I'd still like to win a race for once."

"What about some other kind of race, like biking or running?" Jazz's face broke into a wide grin. "Hey, what about triathlon? You'd be awesome at that!"

"How do you know about triathlon?" Cade asked.

Jazz looked at him, wide-eyed. "Don't you remember Simon Whitfield?"

"Who's he?" Cade asked.

"He won a gold medal in the Sydney Olympics and a silver in Beijing! How have you never heard of him?" Jazz was shocked.

"Wow, I don't know," Cade said.

"Canada's triathletes are very well respected on the international circuit." Jazz looked at her watch and quickly strapped on her helmet and unlocked her mountain bike. "Hey, I have to get going."

The two friends started pedaling for home. They could take the same path, since Jazz only lived a couple of blocks from Cade's house.

"Do you really think I could do it?" he asked, pulling ahead.

"You'll never know unless you try," Jazz said, catching right up.

"Mr. Grimsby said there's a triathlon in two weeks."

"Mr. who?"

"Just some guy I ran into the other day." Cade wasn't about to tell Jazz he had *actually* run into him! "He's already entered the race."

"You should too!" Jazz said.

37

"I was thinking about it. I don't know..."

"Hmm," Jazz said. "Well, we have a month-long break after the Games. And I don't want to get out of shape just lying around the house, watching vampire TV shows and eating potato chips."

"Yeah, like that would ever happen," Cade scoffed.

"So I'll tell you what," she said. "If *you* enter, I'll enter."

"You mean it?"

Jazz nodded.

"Deal," said Cade.

He hadn't known where he was going to find the confidence to sign up for the race. He'd needed someone to tell him to go for it. Someone he could trust. No one at home seemed to care what he did. And he had just met Mr. Grimsby. He was only being friendly. But now Cade realized that the boost he'd needed was riding along right beside him.

"But you're not going to have much time to train for the triathlon when you get back," he said to Jazz.

"Then I guess I better start right now—I'll race you!"

Jazz took off down the path. Cade watched her shoot ahead, weaving in and out of slower riders. She took a fork in the road and zoomed down a trail that wound along the river. Nothing could slow her down. When there were fallen branches on the path, Jazz crouched down, then pulled up her bike and bunny-hopped over the wood. When they came to a hill, she clicked into low gear and spun easily up the steep slope. Cade struggled to keep up. Jazz carved her way around a few more bends until their houses were in sight. Then she put on the brakes and skidded to a stop. Cade kept pedaling as hard as he could until he cruised up beside her.

"With that kind of speed you won't have to do any extra training," he said, gasping for air.

"I said I'd enter with you," Jazz said, laughing. "I never said I'd let you win."

Chapter Seven

Cade glanced at the clock. "Time to roll."

"Where are you off to?" his mom asked, coming into the kitchen. Cade liked that she worked from home as an online travel agent. The previous Christmas, the whole family had flown to Hawaii. Totally awesome!

"Nowhere special," Cade said after swallowing his last mouthful of orange juice.

His mom eyed his clothes. "Hmm. I'm not sure I believe you."

"Oh, you mean what's with the T-shirt, shorts and running shoes?"

"Yes, that's exactly what I mean. Plus, it's not even nine o'clock. These past few days you've been moping around the house. Not shooting out the door like a rocket."

"I'm going to meet someone."

"Jake?"

"No."

"Omar?"

"Nope."

"Jazz?"

"Not today."

"I give up," his mom said. "But please tell me what you're up to. You can't just disappear from the house."

Cade looked down at his feet. He didn't want to answer. He didn't want anyone to know he was about to start training for a triathlon. Especially his dad. He would just give him a hard time. Probably laugh in his face. But his mom had him cornered. Cade knew she'd get the truth out of him eventually. He caved.

"I'm going to meet Mr. Grimsby."

"Old George Grimsby down the street?" she said. "Don't you have any friends your own age you can play with?"

"Go ahead and laugh, Mom. He may be old, but he's in good shape, and he knows a lot about triathlon."

"So that's what he's been doing all these years," she said, nodding. "I've seen him running and biking around the neighborhood, but I had no idea what it was for. Now it all makes sense."

"He said he'd teach me all about it."

"That was nice of him, considering how you met. You know...by accident." His mom grinned at her own wisecrack.

"I'm not in the mood for your lame jokes, Mom."

"Just trying to cheer you up," she said, smiling. "Since when have you been interested in triathlon anyway?"

"Since I came last in my race," he said. "I couldn't believe it, Mom. It made me wonder if I should be swimming at all."

His mom nodded. "I know you took that hard. A new sport might be just what you need. I'm sure your father will agree."

"No he won't. He doesn't think swimming or anything else I do is any good."

His mom shook her head. "That's not true. He's proud of both you and Trent."

"You must be blind," Cade said, throwing up his hands. "All he cares about is Trent and his football. He couldn't care less what I do. Unless I became a star quarterback overnight. And that's not going to happen."

His mom crossed her arms. "Your father just understands football better."

"Why's that? It's not like he was some star player in high school or something."

"Maybe you should ask him sometime," his mom suggested.

"Yeah right," Cade said, rolling his eyes. "I'll just get more excuses about why he likes football so much."

"Well, I still think he'll be impressed when he hears you're training for a triathlon."

She put her arm around Cade's shoulders. "You can tell him when he comes home from work tonight."

Cade shook off her arm. He pushed his chair away from the table and got to his feet. "I'm not going to tell him."

His mom put her hands on her hips. "You shouldn't hide things from your—"

"And you can't tell him either!" Cade blurted out. "You have to keep it a secret. I don't want Dad or Trent to know anything about it. Please, Mom."

Chapter Eight

There was a stand of tall evergreen trees in the park across the street from Mr. Grimsby's house. Cade hid behind them and peeked between the branches. He still wasn't sure the old man wanted to see him. Maybe he'd just felt sorry for him after the bike crash the other day. Finally, he stepped into the open.

"I was hoping you'd make it," Mr. Grimsby said, looking up. He was sitting on his front lawn, stretching his legs.

"Come on over. I was just about to go for a run. You can join me."

"I don't know if I can keep up with you," Cade said.

Mr. Grimsby stared down at Cade's feet. "Not if you're wearing those shoes, you can't."

"What's wrong with them?" Cade asked. "They're my best basketball kicks."

"Last time I checked, basketball shoes were made for shooting hoops, not long-distance running. They're too big and too heavy."

"Oh," Cade said, hanging his head. "I guess I'll run by myself later."

"I have a better idea. Come with me."

Cade followed Mr. Grimsby into his house and down some stairs into the basement.

"Wow!" Cade said, twisting his neck around like an owl. "I've never seen so much sports equipment in one room. Except maybe at a sports store."

Cade could see two racing bikes, one mountain bike, a weight-lifting machine and barbells on the floor. There was even an exercise bike that wouldn't go anywhere no matter how fast you pedaled it.

"Yeah, there's a lot of stuff, all right," Mr. Grimsby called. He was in the next room, searching for something. "But I like to train every day. So if the weather's just too awful, I come down here and put in an hour or two."

Mr. Grimsby came out carrying a big cardboard box. "I'm sure there's a pair of old shoes in here that will fit you." He put the box down and started to rummage through it. "I think we're about the same size."

Cade peered into the box. It was filled with stacks of old running shoes in every color.

"Wow! I've never seen so many."

"I never throw my old shoes away," Mr. Grimsby said, chuckling. "They remind me of the races I ran years ago." Finally he pulled out a bright-red pair. "Here, try these."

Cade laced them up and jogged on the spot to test them out.

"These are a lot lighter and softer than my high-tops, for sure. It's like I'm not wearing shoes at all!"

"Ready to give them a try?"

Cade nodded and grinned.

"Then let's head outside."

When they got to the road, Cade sprinted ahead. He wanted Mr. Grimsby to know he could keep up with him no matter how fast he ran. He didn't want to be left behind like the last time.

"Where's the fire?" Mr. Grimsby called. "Slow down and breathe easy. You don't have to run like a cheetah to improve your fitness."

Cade dropped back beside Mr. Grimsby. He checked his pace and matched him stride for stride.

"That's better."

"How do you know how fast to run?" Cade asked.

"There's a test for that."

Cade swallowed hard. He didn't know he'd have to take a test just to run with Mr. Grimsby. Exams were at the bottom of his list of things he liked about school. Somewhere between doing homework and getting to the bus stop on time.

"It's called the talk test," Mr. Grimsby explained. "As long as you can still carry on a conversation while you're running, you know you're running at the right speed."

Whew! That was one test Cade knew he could pass. He and Mr. Grimsby continued to talk as they ran down into the park. After what didn't seem like long, Mr. Grimsby glanced down at his wrist.

"That's three kilometers. Time to head back."

"How do you know how far we've gone?"

"It's all right here," he said, holding up his black watch. "This baby has a GPS system on it that tells me how far we've run and at what pace. It can even tell me how fast my heart is beating."

"Wow! It's like a mini computer."

"That's exactly what it is."

Mr. Grimsby took an extra-deep breath as they ran over a bridge with the creek rushing beneath them. "There's nothing better than getting out of the house and enjoying nature. Just look around—green grass, leafy trees, blue water."

Cade didn't know what was so special about grass and trees and water. He saw them every day. But he did like being out of the house. "Yeah, sometimes I'd rather not be at home."

"Problems?"

"My dad thinks football is the only sport there is. He thinks I'm a wimp for not playing. But I'm not big enough, like my brother."

"You're plenty big for lots of other sports," Mr. Grimsby said, glancing at Cade. "And triathlon isn't for wimps. You'll see."

"When my dad gets on my case, I just want to walk away." Cade ran for a few more steps and smiled. "At least now I *can* run away."

"I need to get out of the house every so often too," Mr. Grimsby said.

Cade wondered why Mr. Grimsby needed to escape. He was pretty sure he didn't still live with his dad. "Is there someone you want to get away from?"

"Mrs. Grimsby," he said quietly. "But don't get me wrong. She's the sweetest person I know."

"Then why would you need to get away?" Cade asked.

"She doesn't remember who I am."

"She forgets who you are?"

"Yeah, she's got dementia," Mr. Grimsby said. "It's really sad. Takes away all your memories."

Cade thought about what it would be like not to recognize his best friends, like Jazz. "It must be terrible."

"I don't mind taking care of her. I just need some time every day when I'm not worrying about her. So I go for a swim or a run or a bike ride."

The two runners rounded the last bend and headed for home. Cade's legs felt tired, but better than they had when he was wearing his high-tops. These new shoes were awesome. He felt good knowing he had passed the run test too. Talking to Mr. Grimsby had been easy. And he had discovered that they had something more in common than just triathlon.

"Sorry your wife doesn't know who you are," Cade said when they reached his house. "Sometimes I think my dad doesn't know who I am either."

Chapter Nine

"But I don't want to watch the game," Cade complained. "It's boring."

"Boring?" His dad stopped pouring milk on his cereal and stared at him. "I'll tell you what's boring to watch—a swim meet. This is a *football* game. There's nothing more exciting."

On weekday mornings now, Cade waited until his dad left for work and then went running with Mr. Grimsby.

It was paying off too. His legs felt stronger every time out. But today was Saturday. On the weekends, Mr. Grimsby went for bike rides of six hours or longer. There was no way Cade could ride that far, so today Cade had planned to go for a run by himself. His dad had other ideas.

"I've seen Trent play before," Cade said, trying to think of reasons not to go. "What's the big deal?"

"Trent's the star player. Every game's a big deal."

"I'm just the quarterback, Dad," Trent said, joining them at the breakfast table. "Only you think I'm the star."

"Whatever," Cade said. He was tired of all the football talk. "Just go without me."

"You're coming," his dad said, tilting his head at him. "And that's final."

Cade got into the back of the car, clicked his seat belt and crossed his arms. His dad and brother sat in the front. Trent was already dressed for the game in his orange Broncos uniform. His shoulder pads were so big it made it hard for him to get through the car door.

"At least I'll be protected if we ever get into an accident," he joked.

"Maybe you should put on your helmet just in case," Cade said with a laugh. "If it can fit over that big swollen head of yours, that is."

"I don't like joking about those things," his dad said, gripping the wheel. "I've never had an accident and never will. Especially on the way to a game."

It wasn't long before the football chatter started.

"You can beat these guys, Trent."

"I don't know, Dad. The Eagles have a good defense."

"Just remember, the only way to win is to pass."

"But Coach said he wants to run the ball today."

"What does he know?"

"He's been coaching for twenty years," Trent fired back. "And won championships."

"Big deal," his dad said, taking his hand off the steering wheel. "I've been watching football on TV for twenty years. And I've learned a thing or two about winning."

Cade watched Trent turn away from their dad and stare out the window. Whether he was talking about football or swimming, their dad always thought he was right. The car was silent for the rest of the fifteen-minute drive to the field.

As soon as they parked, Trent hopped out and ran to join his teammates on the field. Cade thought this was a good chance to make his escape too. He started to walk away from the car.

"Hey, where do you think you're going?" his dad asked.

"For a walk," Cade said. "I'll be back in time for the game."

"Forget it. You're sticking with me."

Cade followed his dad to the field.

There was a group of parents sitting in the stands near the Broncos bench.

"Look who's here, everyone," one father said. "The star quarterback's dad."

"What did I tell you?" his dad said, elbowing Cade in the ribs. "They think Trent is the best player too."

"Is that the next star quarterback standing beside you, Darrel?" the father asked.

"Who, Cade?" His dad laughed, shaking his head. "No, no, he's just a swimmer. There's only one athlete in the family. And he's on the field."

Cade and his dad found seats near the other Broncos fans. After what seemed like forever, the referee finally blew his whistle to start the game. The Broncos ran back the opening kickoff to their own forty-yard line. Cade saw Trent getting some last-second orders from his coach on the side-line. Then he came running onto the field with the rest of the Broncos offense.

"Let's go, Trent!" his dad shouted.

Trent called the first play. It was a handoff to the running back. The opposing team stopped him cold at the line of scrimmage. There was no gain.

"I can't believe Coach made him call a running play," his dad said loudly. "I told him to pass."

Trent called the second play. It was another run. This time it was a sweep around the left side. The Broncos running back was fast, but the Eagles defense was even faster. He was met by a swarm of defenders. The Broncos runner was tackled after picking up only two yards. It was third down. The Broncos would have to punt the ball to the Eagles.

Cade's dad jumped to his feet. "Coach!" he shouted, cupping his hands together. "That's the dumbest call I've ever seen! You have to pass!"

"Don't worry about it, Darrel," another father said. "It's only the first set of downs. Coach will figure it out."

"Coach doesn't know what he's doing. He's making my boy look bad."

"Sit down," said a mother. "You're blocking my view."

Cade's dad sat down. But only until the Broncos got the ball back. Then he was back on his feet, yelling at Coach again. "Even I'd be a better coach than you!"

The other parents in the crowd started to grumble. Some shifted a few seats farther from where Cade and his dad sat. Cade realized they didn't want to be near him. Cade didn't want to stay there either. It was all totally embarrassing. He felt trapped. He needed to get out of there.

Cade stood up and started toward the stairs.

"Get back here!" his dad shouted. "The game's not over!"

"It is for me."

All the other parents turned their heads to watch. Mothers and fathers gave disapproving looks. Shook their heads. Whispered between themselves.

"Don't expect a ride," his dad replied.

"I don't need one!" Cade shot back.

"It's a pretty long walk."

"I don't care," he said, stepping onto the grass. "And who said I was going to

59

walk anyway?" He didn't know if his dad even heard him. Who cared?

He gave his dad once last angry stare. Then he started to run.

Chapter Ten

Cade pulled back on his handlebars. He popped up his front tire and wheelied down the driveway. He hopped over the curb, tore down the street, then squeezed his brakes, skidding to a stop in front of Mr. Grimsby's house. *Those mountain-bike tricks should impress him.*

"Nice moves," Mr. Grimsby said, kneeling beside his own bike. "There's just one problem."

"What's that?"

"You'll never need them in a triathlon."

"Oh," Cade said. Now he felt stupid for trying to show off.

"It's good that you can control your bike, but triathlon is more about riding straight and long."

"I can do that."

"I bet you can. What do you say we give running a break today and go for a ride?"

"I was hoping you'd say that. I went for a run on the weekend."

"Doing a little extra training?" Mr. Grimsby asked.

"A little more than I had planned," Cade said.

Mr. Grimsby gave Cade an understanding smile. "That's the great thing about being a triathlete. You can always escape. If you don't like the situation you're in, you can just swim, bike or run away from it."

"So what are we waiting for?" Cade asked. He was anxious to get going and leave behind thoughts of his dad.

Mr. Grimsby clipped on his helmet and swung his leg over his sleek bike. "Follow me," he said, rolling down the driveway onto the street. "Just make sure you stay behind me single file. We don't want to get close to any cars."

Cade pulled in right behind Mr. Grimsby. He was stoked for the ride. At first everything went fine. He was able to match Mr. Grimsby's speed. But after a few minutes he had to push harder on his pedals just to keep up. The thing was, it didn't seem like Mr. Grimsby was trying at all. His legs weren't turning anywhere near as fast as Cade's. For every one turn of his pedals, Cade had to take two. It wasn't long before he started to fall behind.

"Wait up!" Cade shouted.

Mr. Grimsby came to a stop and waited for Cade to catch him.

"I'm too slow," Cade groaned.

"I don't think you're too slow. But I think your bike might be."

"What are you talking about? This is a great mountain bike."

"Do you see any mountains around here?" Mr. Grimsby asked, grinning.

Cade looked around—nothing but flat fields as far as he could see. "I guess not."

"Don't worry. I have an idea how to make your bike faster. Let's head back to my house and get to work."

"What's the biggest difference between your bike and mine?" Mr. Grimsby asked, eyeing the two bikes on the driveway.

Cade compared the two. "Mine looks a lot heavier."

"Sure does. Look at those fat, knobby tires. They're great for going down muddy trails and jumping over rocks—"

"But not so great for speeding down paved roads," Cade said.

"You got it." Mr. Grimsby nodded. "And those fenders over the front and rear wheels?"

"What about them?"

"They're just going to weigh you down."

"It would be great to have a special triathlon bike," Cade said. "But I don't think I can afford one."

"No worries," Mr. Grimsby said. "I've got a way to make your bike go faster. And it's free." He rustled around in a box of old biking parts he had brought up from his basement. "Here we go."

Cade watched him pull out two tires. They looked a lot different from his.

"See how smooth and light these are?" Mr. Grimsby asked. "They're called 'slicks'."

"I bet they'd make a bike go a ton faster."

"Let's find out."

Cade helped Mr. Grimsby take off his fat tires and put the smooth ones on. Then they unscrewed the fenders and took them off. It didn't look like a bulky mountain bike anymore. It was a lean, mean triathlon machine.

"Give that a try," Mr. Grimsby said after pumping up the tires.

Cade hopped on and sped along the street. The new tires were like magic. Suddenly his bike was lighter. He could accelerate faster, turn faster and go faster without having to pedal so hard. He felt like he was flying. He came screeching to a stop in front of Mr. Grimsby.

"Awesome!" Cade said.

"That new speed you've got is really going to come in handy during the race. But I noticed your seat was a little low."

"I haven't changed it in a year."

"And you're taller now than you were a year ago. Time for your seat to go up so your legs can stretch out. You'll get the most power that way."

Mr. Grimsby pulled a tool from his pocket. He flicked open a small wrench and adjusted Cade's seat.

"That looks cool," Cade said, looking at the tool.

"Sure is. It's got wrenches, a screwdriver, even a knife. It's tough as nails. Every serious triathlete should have one."

"Oh," Cade said. "I guess I'm not good enough to be serious."

"You are now," Mr. Grimsby said, handing him the pocket tool. "It's all yours."

"Really?"

"Yup. And don't worry. I've got another one."

Cade hopped on his bike again and took it for another short spin.

"The seat is perfect!"

Mr. Grimsby nodded. "Good. You're going to need your bike in perfect condition for the triathlon this weekend. There's going to be a lot of good athletes your age there. You don't want your competitors getting too far ahead."

"I hope I can keep up."

"We'll know soon enough," Mr. Grimsby said, getting on his bike. "See if you can stay with me now."

Cade mounted his own sleek machine. He had been left behind once. With his new wheels, he wasn't going to let it happen again.

Chapter Eleven

"Let's go, Trent!" Cade's dad called.

"What's the rush?" Trent asked as he came down the hall dressed in his Broncos uniform.

"It's an hour's drive to the field. Then you've got to warm up your arm before the game. The star QB can't be late. I'm going to start the car."

"Good luck," Cade said.

"Thanks, bro. You sure you don't want to watch another game?"

"One was enough," Cadc said, shaking his head. "Sorry, man."

"No problem. I know Dad can get a little wound up. But he's my number one fan. He means well."

"And anyway," Cade said, glancing at his mom, "I've got something else going on this morning."

"Is your girlfriend coming over?" Trent teased.

"She's not my girlfriend," Cade said, rolling his eyes. "But yeah, Jazz is coming over."

"Later," Trent said, waving goodbye. "I've got some touchdown passes to throw."

Cade closed the door behind Trent and turned to his mom. "Thanks for not telling dad about my triathlon today."

"This is the last time," she said, pointing her finger at him.

"I know."

"I don't know what you're so worried about, Cade."

"If I do okay at today's race, I can tell him I've been training with Mr. Grimsby. But if I do crappy...then I can just quit triathlon forever. Just like I've quit swimming. Dad never has to know. He never has to tell me I wasn't good enough."

"First of all," his mom said, meeting his eyes, "you haven't quit swimming—you're just taking a break to try something new. And second, you're not out to win the race. You're out to have fun." Her face warmed into a smile. "Besides, I'm sure you'll do fine."

"I know you're just saying that."

"No, I mean it. I've seen how hard you've been training." She peered out the window. "So when's George coming by to take you and Jazz to the triathlon?"

"Any minute."

Cade heard a skid on the driveway and looked out the window. It was Jazz, right on time. She was carrying a backpack and pedaling a road bike Cade hadn't seen before.

"Hey, buddy!" Jazz called out.

"Hey! Haven't seen you since you got back from the Games," Cade said, grinning.

"Yeah, sorry about that. I've been so busy. My relatives keep coming over to see me."

"No kidding," Cade said. "It's not every day they get to see a famous triple medalist."

"It was no biggie," Jazz said.

"No big deal?" Cade said, his eyes wide with excitement. "You won *three* medals—a gold and two bronze!"

"I could have had a fourth one in the 200 fly." Jazz shrugged. "But I had a bad turn on the last lap and got touched out at the wall by a swimmer from Ontario."

"How did it feel to be on the podium?"

"Pretty sweet, I have to admit." Jazz smiled.

Cade nodded. "I can only imagine." *Standing higher than anyone else. Knowing you were the best. Hearing Coach and your teammates cheer. Seeing your parents in the crowd, being proud of you.*

Cade realized he was thinking more about himself than Jazz. "You must be wiped out from all the swimming."

"And don't forget all the visiting," she added.

"I wouldn't have blamed you for not showing up this morning."

"I said I was in, so I'm in. I wouldn't let you down, Cade. But I haven't had time to run or ride much. I'm even borrowing a bike. I'm sure I'll finish last."

"Where'd you get the bike?" Cade asked, scoping out her ride.

"It's my brother's road bike," Jazz said. "It's lighter and has skinnier tires than my mountain bike, so it goes way faster."

"You got that right. Mr. Grimsby helped me trick out my bike so it goes faster too."

Jazz picked up her backpack. "Got your race kit?"

"Yup, picked it up yesterday." We had all gotten an orange swim cap. And a timing chip to wrap around our ankles to record our times for the race.

"I thought this was the coolest thing," Jazz said, pulling a blue T-shirt from her pack and holding it up. *Official Calgary Triathlon Finisher*, it read.

"I'm not wearing mine until I finish—if I finish," Cade said, hesitating. "Might be bad luck."

"Don't worry. You're going to rock this race."

A toot of the horn announced Mr. Grimsby's arrival. He pulled his car into the driveway and hopped out.

"So you must be Jazz," he said, smiling. "I hear you're quite the swimmer."

"Today I hope I'm a biker and runner as well," Jazz said.

Mr. Grimsby glanced at his special triathlon watch. "We should be on our way."

"Let's get our bikes loaded," Cade said, strapping first his and then Jazz's bike onto the rack on the back of the car.

"Almost ready to head out, George?" Cade's mom asked as she came down the walkway.

"Yup, we're going to have a great day. Cade is really starting to round into form."

"Thanks to you, George."

"It's been fun having someone to train with."

"How's Sadie doing?" she said, changing the subject.

"Oh, pretty much the same," he said. "She has her good days and then not-so-good ones. I've arranged for a nurse to come in today."

"You're a good man, George," she said. "Thanks for taking Cade under your wing. His father doesn't seem to care about any sport other than football. But I wish he did."

"He's a great kid. It's a short sprint race today, and the lake is close by. I'll have him back this afternoon."

Chapter Twelve

The start gun boomed. The Calgary Triathlon had begun.

Cade and Jazz dashed through the shallow part of the lake. Their bare feet kicked up white spray as they ran toward deeper water. The hot sun warmed the cool splashes on their skin.

Athletes wearing orange swim caps were all around them. Hundreds of kids of all ages charged through the surf. They all had numbers marked on their bodies.

Cade had a black *1425* drawn on his arm and his leg. That meant he was entered in the fourteen-year-old division for boys. Jazz had *1426*, but she was in the girls' group. They both had their timing chips strapped to their left ankles.

Now the water was up to their waists. Deep enough for them to dive in and start swimming. Cade and Jazz plunged at the same time, but it wasn't long before Jazz started to pull away.

At first Cade tried to keep up. But he soon realized he should swim at his own pace. Jazz was just too speedy. He slowed down and caught his breath. That felt better. Maybe he could catch up with her on the bike or run.

Whack! A sharp pain cracked the side of Cade's head. He had been kicked by a swimmer in front of him. The other swimmer had no idea Cade was right behind him. But with so many athletes packed together like sardines in a can, accidents were bound to happen. Cade shook it off and kept going.

The swim for this triathlon was 500 meters. That was like doing twenty laps of the pool. Cade had done that every morning while he was training with the Blue Sharks. Sometimes even more. He knew he could do the distance. But swimming in a lake was a lot different. For one thing, there were no lanes.

He was aiming for the big yellow buoy floating in the middle of the lake. It was shaped like a pyramid and marked the halfway point of the swim. He lifted his head and peered through his goggles to make sure he was on target. But he was way off course! He had veered close to one of the safety kayaks. The paddlers were there just in case a swimmer needed help. He put his head down and turned to get back on track. He had lost valuable seconds. He churned through the water a little faster to make up for lost time.

Cade rounded the buoy and headed back to shore. He had made a good recovery. He shot a glance to his left and then to his right. There were only a few swimmers ahead of him. One was a girl way out in front. He knew who that must be.

He powered through the water, keeping his breathing even. He looked up every once in a while to make sure he was still heading for the finish.

A minute later he was in shallow water again. As soon as he could, he stood up and splashed toward the sandy beach. The spectators cheered him on. He raced by a big digital clock that read *11:37*. It had taken him a lot longer than it would have taken him in the pool. But Mr. Grimsby said any time under twelve minutes was good in a lake. Cade sprinted to the transition area.

There were long rows of bikes all lined up in racks. Cade had placed his there before the race, along with the clothes he'd need for the ride. His heart was still racing as he found his bike and started to change. His bathing suit now became his biking shorts. It was soaking wet, but he knew it would dry as he rode. He pulled on a T-shirt and socks and then laced up the red running shoes Mr. Grimsby had given him.

He strapped on his helmet and was ready to go.

He glanced at the other athletes getting their bikes. He knew Jazz was long gone. But that didn't matter—she was in the girls' division. Two boys with numbers on their arms starting with *14* were hopping on their bikes. Did that mean he was in third place? He wondered if he could catch them. He pushed his bike to the start of the second stage and jumped on.

The biking stage of the triathlon was ten kilometers. That was a long way for Cade to ride. He had covered the distance with Mr. Grimsby in training, but never at top speed. He hoped he could make it while going all out.

He stepped down on the pedals and took off. The race route was along the streets of Calgary. Luckily, he didn't have to worry about traffic. The police were there to block all the cars. He could safely ride down the middle of the roads.

Cade chased after the bike in front of him. He leaned over his handlebars to stay low.

He knew that was the best way to keep up his speed against the wind. The new slick tires were lightning quick. The frame without fenders was feather light. His wheels spun faster than ever. He shot by the halfway sign still feeling strong.

Cade's confidence started to grow. Maybe Jazz was right. Maybe triathlon *was* his sport. He may not have been the best swimmer, biker or runner. But he was better than average at all three. A big grin started to spread across his face.

Maybe a bit too soon. Another competitor suddenly flew by him on the left. His hands were gripped low on his handlebars. His powerful legs cranked on the pedals. His eyes were hidden behind dark sunglasses. Cade checked his number...1487! In the blink of an eye Cade had slipped from third to fourth place. He was off the podium. *Here we go again*.

Chapter Thirteen

Cade wondered how 1487 could have passed him so easily. Flown by him like a fighter jet. Then he took a closer look at his bike. It was an aerodynamic model similar to Mr. Grimsby's. Cade knew it was made with carbon fiber, so it was super light. Plus, it had a ton of big gears to go fast. And it was going fast. He was pulling away. Cade didn't know if his fixed-up mountain bike could catch him. But he was going to try. He pushed forward. He wasn't going down without a fight.

There wasn't much farther to go in the bike stage. Cade wanted to catch the third-place rider before the next transition area. He put his head down and attacked the pedals. *Push...push...push!* His thighs burned with pain. His hands gripped the handlebars. He was gaining on the boy who had passed him. He just needed a few more seconds to get even with him. Then he looked up. A man was wildly waving his arms. It was a race official.

"Slow down, 1425!" the man shouted.

Cade had been biking so hard, he hadn't noticed how close he was to the end of the stage. If he didn't come to a stop before the next transition area, he'd be disqualified. He wasn't allowed to cross the white line while he was still on his bike. He squeezed his brake handles hard. His front and back wheels locked up, sending the bike into a wild skid that left a snaking black tire mark on the road. When the sound of squealing brakes was over, Cade's bike had stopped just a hair short of the line.

He hopped off and pushed his bike back to the rack. He noticed the other boy had already parked his bike and was hustling toward the start of the run stage. Cade didn't have a second to lose. He unclipped his helmet and tossed it by his bike. Then he bolted.

The run was four kilometers long. Four heart-pounding kilometers to pass the athlete in front of him. Cade couldn't wait. He sprinted to try and reel him in. Number 1487 was in his sights. If he just pushed a little harder, he could do it. His chest heaved. His breaths came short and fast. Too fast. He remembered what Mr. Grimsby had said. *Pace yourself*. He slowed down. He still had time to catch him.

Even though he was running step for step with the third-place boy, he wasn't able to reach him. He was still twenty meters ahead. But he was gaining on another athlete. As he rounded the next bend in the road he spotted a girl running ahead. Jazz. A few seconds later he was even with her.

"You're the lead girl!" Cade said, turning his head.

"I know, but I'm running out of gas," Jazz panted.

"Hang in there," Cade encouraged. "You can do it!"

Cade knew Jazz had been ahead of him all the time. She was an awesome swimmer. And an amazing bike rider. But she hadn't had enough time to prepare for the run. It was no surprise she was tired. If this had been a training run, he would have stayed with her to the end. But he was on a mission. With a last "Keep going!" he turned his head straight and left Jazz behind. He glued his eyes on the boy ahead and pushed on. If he was going to catch him, it was now or never.

Less than a kilometer to go. Not just in the run but in the whole triathlon. He picked up his pace. His legs kicked faster. His arms pumped harder. His heart thumped like it would jump out of his chest. He knew he couldn't keep this up for long. But he had to for just long enough. He was closing in.

The race banner that hung across the road was dead ahead. *CALGARY TRIATHLON FINISH.* Just a hundred meters to go. Now he was shoulder to shoulder with the third-place runner. The boy shot a glance at him. He was still wearing dark sunglasses. But he didn't look so cool and calm. His face was dripping sweat. His mouth was wide open, trying to suck in as much oxygen as possible. He groaned with every breath.

Cade thought he had him. The other boy was fading fast. There was no way he could speed up. In a few steps Cade would pass him, and it would all be over. He smiled. Cade imagined himself on the podium. Getting the third-place medal. Hearing the crowd cheer him. Telling his dad he was a winner. That he had finally found a sport he was good at. Just like Trent.

He snapped back to attention. The finish line was just a stride away. He squeezed every ounce of energy out of his tired body and lunged forward. He stepped on the pad. He heard a beep. Then another beep.

Cade sprawled on the ground. His legs were too weak to take one more step. But he didn't have to. The race was over. All the pain was worth it. He was sure he had come third. Hadn't he?

He looked up. A race official was patting the other boy on the back. He checked his number and name on a clipboard "Nice job...Adam. You held on for third place."

Cade couldn't believe it. He closed his eyes. He stayed slumped on the ground.

The race official kneeled down beside him. "Fourth place isn't so bad...Cade. You just missed the podium."

"I've been missing it for a long time," Cade said.

Chapter Fourteen

Cade's parents were waiting for him on the driveway. He had texted earlier to let them know he was almost home. He eased himself out of the car with Jazz and Mr. Grimsby. He was still tired from the race.

"How'd it go?" his mom asked, smiling.

"Well, I finished," Cade said slowly. He was still mad at himself for losing his focus and letting the other guy finish ahead of him.

"He didn't just finish," Jazz piped up. "He finished fourth!"

"You came fourth?" his mom asked, rushing over to give him a hug.

Cade pushed her away. He didn't want to be treated like a little kid in front of his friends.

"You should have seen your son out there," Mr. Grimsby said. "The way he swam, biked and ran. It was like he'd been competing for years. You would have been proud."

Everybody had big smiles on their faces. Except for one. Cade's father stood with his hands on his hips. He looked stone-cold. "Why didn't you tell me about the race?" he demanded.

"I don't know."

"Did you forget?"

"No."

"Then what was it?" His father's eyes narrowed to slits.

"I didn't think you'd care," Cade said, staring at his shoes, too afraid to look up.

"You're right—I don't care," his father said, stabbing the air with his finger. "Not when I find out like this. Not when your mother tells me just a few minutes ago.

Not when you've kept all this a secret from me for weeks."

Mr. Grimsby spoke up. "I think Cade thought you might have been too busy with football. I hear Trent is a fine quarterback."

"Yeah, he's a star, all right. He's got *pro* written all over him. And he's playing a *real* sport."

"Triathlon is a real sport too," Mr. Grimsby said.

"Try-a-thon...try-a-long...Whatever it's called, it's not like football, that's for sure. You should have been at this morning's game. I bet there were a hundred fans cheering Trent on."

"That's nothing," Jazz said, staring down Cade's father. Cade couldn't believe it. "There must have been a thousand people at the triathlon—competitors, parents, officials, reporters, even TV cameras. After my event I took a video of the whole thing with my phone. I'll post it on YouTube. You'll see for yourself." Jazz took a big step toward Cade's dad. Her eyes were blazing. "And you know what the big crowd saw?

They saw Cade give everything he had. They saw him miss third place by a split second. He was almost on the podium. It was an amazing performance. You've got two star athletes in your family, Mr. Dixon. Not just one."

Jazz took a step back so she was beside Cade and Mr. Grimsby. Now all three of them stood in a line across from Cade's father.

"You have to admit, fourth place is pretty impressive," Cade's mom said.

"Maybe it is. Maybe it isn't," Cade's father said, crossing his arms. "I have nothing to compare it to. So. How did you do, Jazz?"

Cade got the feeling his dad already knew the answer.

"It doesn't matter how I did," she said.

"I think it does matter," Cade's father said.

Jazz paused before answering. "I did okay."

"How okay?"

"I came first," she said quietly.

"First? That's what I thought," Cade's father said, his voice growing louder. "Sounds like anybody can win a gold medal. Finishing fourth is no big deal."

"The Calgary Triathlon organizers thought it was a real achievement," Mr. Grimsby said. "They invited the top five finishers to the Alberta Championship in Sylvan Lake two weeks from now."

Cade's father faked a laugh. "You've got to be joking if you think I'm going to drive Cade two hours all the way to Sylvan Lake. He'll do even worse in that race. Besides, Trent's got football."

"I'll be competing at Sylvan Lake myself," Mr. Grimsby said. "I'd be happy to drive him and Jazz to the race."

"Thank you for the kind offer, George," Cade's mom said. "I think it would be great if Cade could compete in a big race like that." She gave a quick sideways glance at Cade's dad. "Darrel and I will talk it over. We'll let you know if Cade is going."

Cade lifted two bikes down from the rack and waved as Mr. Grimsby backed the car out of the driveway. He turned and wheeled his bike straight toward the open garage, not even looking at his friend before calling out, "See you later, Jazz."

"Where do you think you're going?" his father said.

"The only place I'm allowed to go," Cade fired back. "Inside the house!"

"Get back here right now," his father ordered.

"Why?" Cade said, holding his ground. "So you can tell me I can't go to the next triathlon? So you can tell me I'm not good enough? Or so you can tell me about Trent's next big game? Which one, Dad? Or maybe it's all three?"

Cade pushed his bike into the dark garage. Then he disappeared behind the closing door.

Chapter Fifteen

"Are you going over to Mr. Grimsby's this morning?" Cade's mom was in a cheery mood. The exact opposite of Cade. He sat slumped on a stool at the kitchen island. His bowl of cereal was getting soggy.

"What's the point?" Cade asked. "Dad probably won't ever let me enter another triathlon."

"He was just surprised to find out that way. It was my fault. I should have told him before."

"He sure was mad," Cade said.

"He calmed down after I explained everything to him last night."

"So I can go to the one in Sylvan Lake?"

"You sure can."

"Really?" he said. "Do you think you guys could come and watch me?"

His mom pursed her lips. "I wish we could, but Dad has to take Trent to his game that day. We only have the one car, and it can't be in two places at once."

"Figures! All Dad cares about is Trent and his stupid football."

"That's not true," his mom said.

"Then why doesn't he take me and let someone else on the Broncos take Trent?"

His mom didn't answer right away. "Well, your dad agreed that it would be good for Mr. Grimsby to take you."

Cade wasn't buying it. He knew his dad still thought Trent's football was a lot bigger deal than his triathlon. But at least he was allowed to go. Besides, Mr. Grimsby was a lot more fun to hang out with than his dad was.

"I guess I'll take off," Cade said, picking up his helmet. "We've still got a lot of training to do. I have to practice keeping my focus right until the end of the race."

"Don't forget your grandparents are coming for dinner tonight," his mom said. "They're driving down this afternoon. So make sure you're home by five o'clock."

Cade's mom always seemed to get tense when they came for a visit. Especially if Grandpa wasn't in a good mood, which was most of the time.

"You boys are getting so big," Grandma said. She stood between her grandsons with one hand high on each of their shoulders.

"Just eating my vegetables," Trent joked.

"And you're going to eat some more tonight," their mom said. "Dinner is ready. The ham is on the table. Everyone have a seat, please."

"I can't believe how much you've grown since last time we saw you," Grandma said again, passing a plate of buns around the table. "Now when was that?"

"I think it was a few months ago, when you came to my first game of the season," Trent said.

"Oh yeah, that was quite a game," Grandpa said, lighting up. "You threw for three touchdowns! I sure felt proud watching you. It brought back a lot of memories of when I was a quarterback in high school. Dead-Eye Dixon, they used to call me. It's nice that someone else in the family is finally becoming a good football player."

"Your son played football too, don't forget," Grandma said, smiling over at Cade's dad at the head of the table.

"I'm still trying to forget," Grandpa said. "I'm not sure you can call what he played football. He was the worst pass receiver I've ever seen. Couldn't catch a ball if there was glue on his fingers."

"I'm sure Dad could catch one of my passes," Trent said. "They're always right on the money."

"He couldn't have been that bad," Cade said, surprised he was taking his dad's side. He was still mad at him, but he knew no one liked to be put down.

"Are you kidding?" Grandpa said. "I went to the first few games, but then I quit going. It was too embarrassing."

"Well, you don't have to be good at football to be good in business," Grandma said, turning to Cade's dad. "Did you get that promotion at work you've been hoping for, Darrel?"

Cade's dad shook his head. "No, they gave it to someone else. I couldn't believe it. I never get a break."

"I'm sure they'll recognize your talent soon," Grandma said.

"You've got to be good at something before they recognize you for it," Grandpa said. "It doesn't sound like you're much better at business than you were at football. You better pull up your socks, son."

Cade glanced at his dad. He looked sad. Like he had been beat up. But he hadn't been hit by punches, just nasty words. Cade wondered how his grandpa could be so mean. And realized how hard it must have been for his dad growing up. Never being good enough for him.

That's why football was such a big deal to his dad. It was because football was such a big deal to *his* dad—to Grandpa. Cade's dad wanted Trent to be the star that he never was. Maybe that would make Grandpa feel good about Trent *and* his dad.

But Cade didn't think things would ever change. His dad would probably always be trying to impress Grandpa. He'd always be more interested in Trent's football than whatever Cade was into. Cade knew that if he wanted to be good at triathlon, there was only one person in the family he could depend on—himself.

Chapter Sixteen

Just one week to go. Just seven more days to get ready for the Alberta Championship Triathlon. A few more training sessions to make sure his swimming was smooth, his biking powerful and his running as fast as it could be all the way to the finish. Now that Jazz had gone back to swimming full time, it would be just Cade and Mr. Grimsby. He headed out the front door and sprinted down the street to Mr. G.'s house.

There was no sense walking. Every run would help his conditioning.

But Mr. Grimsby wasn't outside waiting for him as usual. He wasn't stretching on his lawn, getting ready for a run. He wasn't oiling the chain on his bike. He was nowhere to be seen. *That's weird.*

Cade walked up to the front door. He noticed all the curtains were pulled tight. He rang the doorbell. No answer. He rang it again. Finally, just as he was about to walk away, the door swung open. Mr. Grimsby stood there, still in his pajamas.

"Oh, hi! Are you feeling okay?" Cade asked.

"No, I've had better days," Mr. Grimsby said, smiling weakly. He looked like he hadn't slept. Strands of gray hair flopped over his forehead. For the first time, Mr. Grimsby acted as if he really was old— not strong and full of energy like usual.

Mr. Grimsby wasn't sniffling or coughing like Cade did when he got sick. "So...you caught a cold? Or the flu?"

"No, it's more serious than that."

"Is there something I can get for you to make you feel better?"

"I'm afraid there's no cure for what I have."

Cade gulped. "What have you got?"

"A broken heart," Mr. Grimsby said.

Cade wasn't sure what he meant. Mr. Grimsby's heart seemed in good shape. Cade was always the one huffing and puffing, trying to keep up.

"Mrs. Grimsby died last night," he said quietly. "She didn't even remember me in the end."

Cade didn't know what to say. "Oh."

"So I won't be running with you today."

"That's okay," Cade said. "It can wait until tomorrow."

"I'm afraid I won't be able to train with you at all this week. A lot of friends and family will be coming to visit. And I have to get ready for her funeral on the weekend."

"Next weekend?" Cade asked, wrinkling his brow. "But that's the triathlon!"

"I know," Mr. Grimsby said. "I won't be able to drive you to Sylvan Lake. I'm sorry."

"Oh. That's okay." As Mr. Grimsby started to close the door, he added, "I'm sorry about Mrs. Grimsby."

"Thank you, son." Mr. Grimsby paused and then said, "Remember, Cade, you can do this. I've tried to teach you all that I know. You've done the training. Now you just have to believe in yourself."

Cade turned and walked slowly home. He felt really bad for Mr. Grimsby. But now how was he going to get to the triathlon?

When Cade walked into the house, his mom could tell something was wrong. He told her about Mrs. Grimsby.

"Poor old George," his mom said.

"And me," Cade said.

"What do you mean?" his mom asked.

Cade knew his problem was small compared to Mr. Grimsby's, but still. "Now I can't go to the triathlon."

"Let's see what your father says."

They walked out to the backyard, where Trent and his dad were tossing the football around. Cade's mom explained what had happened.

"I told you," Cade's dad said, shaking his head, "Trent has a big game that weekend."

"Forget it, mom. It's fine."

"Actually, though, there's one way you could get to Sylvan Lake," his dad said.

"What's that?" Cade hadn't thought there was any way his dad would consider driving him. But even if there was a one-in-a-million chance, he wanted to know what it was.

"Red Deer is right next to Sylvan Lake. If Trent's team ends up playing against Red Deer in the final, we could drop you off."

"But Red Deer will never win," Trent said. "They're playing against Edmonton today in the semifinal. They're a powerhouse."

"But sometimes the underdog wins, right?" Cade said. "Sometimes the small guy comes out on top?"

Trent shrugged. "I guess it's possible."

"Yeah, but don't get your hopes up," his dad said. "My money's on Edmonton."

"I have a friend in Edmonton who's at the game right now," Trent said, pulling his phone out of his jeans. He quickly thumbed a message. A few seconds later his phone buzzed. His eyes bugged out of his head. "I can't believe it."

"What?" Cade asked.

"Check it out," he said, holding up the phone for Cade and his dad to read. "Final score."

Red Deer 21–Edmonton 20

Chapter Seventeen

"Grandma says they're all set for our visit," Cade's dad said, reading a text message.

He was in the front passenger seat. Cade's mom was behind the wheel. Cade and Trent sat in the back, playing games on their phones.

His dad turned his head toward them. "She says it's just a fifteen-minute drive to the football field." Cade's grandparents lived in the town of Blackfalds, just north of Red Deer.

"All right!" Trent said. "We can get to my ten o'clock game tomorrow no sweat."

"But how far is it to Sylvan Lake for the triathlon?" Cade asked.

"I didn't ask," his dad said.

"Why not? I have to be there by seven to put my bike into the transition area." His bike was strapped to the rack that Mr. Grimsby had lent them for the trip.

"That's pretty early," his dad said.

"You guys know I have to be there first thing! To make sure my gear's all set up and my bike seat's adjusted," he said, holding up his bike tool.

"Don't worry," his mom said. "I can drop you off early. Then I'll drive back to Blackfalds and pick up Trent and go watch his game."

"Who's going to watch me?" Cade asked, not expecting an answer. He pulled his hoodie over his head and stared out the window as the sky began to darken.

After driving for an hour and a half, his mom tapped the dashboard. "Looks like we're getting low on gas."

"Let's take the next exit and fill up in Red Deer," his dad said. "It's just off the highway."

They drove through the small city in silence, through the downtown area, past the shopping mall, the hospital. Cade watched the red Emergency sign flicker in the dark.

I'm going to pull in at that station."

"Why don't I drive the rest of the way?" his dad said, hopping out at the pumps.

"Are you sure?" his mom asked.

"No problem. It's getting late, and I know a shortcut my parents take."

Cade checked his watch. It was already ten o'clock. Were they ever going to get there? He needed to get a good night's sleep.

His dad filled the tank and slipped into the driver's seat. Then they were off.

"We'll take this backroad to Blackfalds," he said, turning off the main route. "It goes over the Blindman River. Not a lot of people know about it. But it will save us a few minutes."

The car sped down the dark road. Cade cracked the window open. He could hear rushing water not far away. "The river sounds fast."

His mom nodded. "Must be all the rain we had last week."

"There's the bridge," his dad said, proud that he had found the way.

"Watch out!" his mom screamed.

"What?"

"There's an animal on the bridge!"

Cade's dad yanked hard on the steering wheel. But he was too late.

WHACK!!!

The car crashed into the deer and swerved to the right. The brakes squealed. The tires skidded. They hurtled sideways toward the edge of the bridge.

The car flew through the air like a terrifying ride at an amusement park. But this ride was for real. Down...down...down they plunged, toward the river.

"Hold on!" yelled Cade's dad.

All Cade could see was blackness. All he could hear were the screams from his family.

The car hit the water with a thunderous jolt. Cade lurched forward but was saved by his seat belt. The front end of the car started to sink first. The hood began to disappear into the murky, black water.

Cade looked down. Water was already bursting through the floor of the car.

"We have to get out!"

"I'm stuck!" his mom shouted.

"Unbuckle your seat belt," Cade said. He tried to remain calm. He breathed deeply like it was the end of a grueling race.

"My window won't open!" Trent shouted, flicking the electric switch

"The battery's dead," his dad said. "There's no power."

His mom pushed against the side of the car. "My door is jammed!"

"There's too much water pressure from the river!" his dad yelled. "We'll have to break a window!"

The water was rising. Swirling black liquid was now up to Cade's waist. It was cold.

He started to shiver. They all pounded against the windows with their hands. It was no use.

"Wait!" Cade cried. "I have an idea." He pulled the bike tool from his pocket. He opened the screwdriver and held it firmly in his fist. The pointed steel blade poked through his fingers. Then he punched the window with all his strength. A small crack appeared. He punched again and again until the glass broke and water started to pour in.

"Everyone has to go through this window!" he said, knocking glass out of the way. "Mom, you first!"

Water had crested their shoulders. Cade's mom took a deep breath and floated to the backseat. She wriggled through the opening like a fish. Cade's dad and Trent had wider shoulders. Cade had to push them through, one at a time.

Cade felt the car hit bottom. The river had almost filled the car. Water coiled around Cade's neck like a noose. In a few seconds he wouldn't be able to breathe.

He took one last gulp of air and pulled himself through the window. Then he disappeared into the dark chill of the Blindman River.

Chapter Eighteen

Which way was up? Cade didn't know. The car had sunk to the bottom of the dark river. There was no sunlight to guide his way to the surface. He might as well have been blind. He floated limply through the frigid water. His eyes darted around in panic. He could only hold his breath for a few more seconds. Where was his family? Which way was up?

Then he saw it. The light from the moon filtering down through the blackness.

He reached up his arms and swam toward the faint glow.

His head popped out of the water like a cork. He gasped for air. He looked around desperately.

"Mom! Dad! Trent!"

His cries were swallowed up by the sound of the rushing river. But then he heard a faint cry.

"We're over here!"

He swam in the direction of the voice. His wet clothes hugged his body. His shoes were tied tightly on his feet. He couldn't get rid of them even if he wanted to. He moved slowly through the water, like he was swimming in a straitjacket. He put one arm in front of the other and kept going. A few strokes later he saw them. His mom and dad were clinging to each other in the middle of the river. They had found a rock and were holding on.

"Your dad can't make it to the shore," his mom said.

"It's my arm!" Cade's dad said, wincing.

Cade saw the huge gash on his father's arm, just above the elbow. He must have been cut squeezing through the window.

"Can you make it to shore, Mom?"

"I think so. But I'm not leaving your father."

"Don't worry, I'll help him. Did you see Trent?"

"No!" his mom said. Her eyes were wide, terrified. "You know he's not a strong swimmer."

"I'll find him. But we've got to get you safe first."

Cade's mom started to swim to shore while Cade gently pulled his father from the rock and eased him into the water. "Relax, Dad. Just float on your back." He put one arm across his dad's chest and used his other arm to swim sidestroke. *It's a good thing I took all those life-saving drills in swimming lessons.*

His dad choked as water washed over his face. "How much farther?"

"Almost there."

A few strokes later Cade was able to stand on the rocky bottom. His father leaned on him as they waded through the shallow water to the riverbank.

His mom was already there, waiting for them. She had ripped a strip of fabric from her shirt and held it in one hand. "I'll tie this around his arm to stop the bleeding. You've got to find Trent!"

"I know. I will."

Cade looked out over the river and cupped his hands together around his mouth.

"Treeent! Treeeeeeeeeent!"

There was no answer.

His brother was a great football player but a lousy swimmer. He had never wanted to take lessons.

Cade was so cold now he was having trouble moving. But he had to find his brother. He left his parents sitting together in the shadow of the bridge. He launched himself back into the deep darkness like he was diving from the starting blocks. The race to save his brother was on.

He swam toward the middle of the river. His arms pulled strongly by his sides. His legs kicked smoothly behind him. Every few strokes he would look up, trying to catch sight of Trent. The same way he searched for the buoy in the triathlon.

He let the current carry him downstream, hoping that was what had happened to Trent. At least his brother could float. The moonlight reflected off the water. An eerie glow spread across the river. Long branches cast spooky shadows across the water. He called again.

Nothing. And then, very faintly, he heard it.

"Cade!"

Trent's voice sounded like it was coming from the edge. Cade spotted some old trees that had fallen into the water along the riverbank.

"I'm stuck in the trees!"

Cade swam faster than he had in any race. The current was strong and tried to sweep him away, but he kept swimming.

His arms powered through the water until he was at his brother's side.

"I never thought you'd find me," Trent said weakly. He was hanging on to a big log. Only his head and hands were above the water. He had been in the water a long time. Cade knew his body temperature must be getting dangerously low.

"We have to get you to shore. You have to get warm."

"Okay," Trent whispered. He was too tired to say any more.

"Hold on to me."

Trent reached out his arm. His big football frame floated beside his smaller brother. Cade pulled him toward the riverbank like a tugboat guiding a ship safely into port.

Trent lay on the shore, too worn out to move. "Where are mom and dad?"

"They're upriver. We have to get back to them."

"I don't know if I can make it," he said, trying to stand.

"Lean on me. You can do it."

Trent hung one arm over Cade's shoulder. The two brothers stumbled through the woods along the riverbank. Their clothes were dripping wet, their shoes soggy from the water. Prickly plants and bushes scratched their arms and legs. But they trudged on through the moonlit trees.

"I'm done," Trent gasped, falling to the ground.

"There's the bridge!" Cade said, picking him up. "We're almost there."

Chapter Nineteen

"Trent!"

Cade's mom leaped to her feet and hugged Trent. "We thought we had lost you," she said, wiping tears away.

"Cade saved me," Trent said, still leaning against his brother.

"He rescued us too," his mom said, sitting back down beside their dad. "We were clinging to a rock. We'd be washed away by now if it wasn't for him."

Cade eased Trent to the ground beside his parents. "Dad doesn't look so good," he said.

"He needs a doctor," his mom said.

"We can't call for help," Trent said. "Our cell phones are at the bottom of the river. There are no cars driving by. No one is going to find us this late at night."

"I never should have taken that shortcut," his dad groaned.

"How could you have known a deer would be on the bridge?" Cade said, shaking his head. "It wasn't your fault."

"Looks like we'll have to wait until the sun comes up," Trent said, staring up at the moon.

"I don't know if your dad will make it until morning," his mom said. She held his injured arm in her lap. "He's losing a lot of blood."

"We're not waiting until morning," Cade said, standing up.

"What do you mean?" his mom asked.

"I'm going to get help."

"How?"

"My bike fell off the back of the car as we crashed through the railing. I'll go find it and ride into town. I remember we passed a hospital."

"That must be twenty kilometers back!" his mom cried.

"Yeah, but we need help now," Cade said, glancing around the forest. "You three need to stay as warm as you can. Maybe Trent can build a shelter with some branches. Then all three of you can huddle together inside. But don't worry—I'll be back."

He made his way up the side of the steep bank, grasping the rocks and small trees as he climbed. Streetlights shone down on the bridge high above him. The rest of the road stretched out into darkness.

He scanned the bridge. The deer lay lifeless on the black pavement. A trickle of blood oozed from its mouth. It must have died instantly. He felt sorry for the animal and wondered briefly whether other members of its family were nearby. But then he spotted his bike. It was scratched up pretty bad. The chain was off. He picked up the wreckage and inspected the damage. The wheels and pedals were in good shape, but the handlebars and seat were badly twisted. Nothing that a handy bike tool couldn't fix, he thought. He pulled the tool from his pocket, glad he had kept it after smashing the window.

A short time later Cade hopped on, anxious to get moving. He pushed a few times on the pedals, but his legs felt heavy and sore. He had no power. All that swimming in the cold river had tired him out. But then he realized it was just like finishing a triathlon swim and shifting to the bike stage of the race. It would take a while for his leg muscles to loosen up. Mr. Grimsby had taught him to expect that. He relaxed, knowing his strength would return. It had to. His dad's life depended on it.

Cade stepped down hard on the pedals. Now he was grateful his running shoes hadn't fallen off in the river. Riding in bare feet would have been painful. And slow.

He shot forward into the night. Past the tall oaks casting moonlit shadows across the road. Past the crickets chirping in the fields. Past the raccoons staring glassy-eyed from the woods. Past the sign that said *Red Deer 10 km*. His wheels spun silently beneath him. There were no other competitors to worry about. No spectators to cheer him on. He was alone.

He was making good time. But he needed to go faster. Every minute counted.

Now he was on the edge of town. There were streetlights to guide his way. He sped by a gas station and a 7-Eleven. His throat was dry. He swallowed hard and imagined how good a Big Gulp would taste right now.

Soon there were more signs of life. Houses. Buildings. Restaurants. And another sign. The one he had been hoping to see—*Hospital 5 km*. He was closing in on his goal. He shifted into a higher gear and put his head down. He was almost there.

There was a sharp bend in the road ahead. He wouldn't let that slow him down. He pedaled hard and leaned into the corner.

But something was wrong. He felt his wheels starting to slip. He looked down. There was oil on the road! His wheels slid out from beneath him. Cade sailed through the air and slammed onto the blacktop. Hard. He skidded along the rough pavement, over what felt like broken glass or sharp stones. He could feel the skin ripping off his arms and legs. He cried out in pain. After a couple of somersaults he tumbled into a ditch.

He lay there dazed. His head was woozy from the crash, his body crumpled in a ball. He slowly unwound, one arm, one leg at a time. He sat up. He knew his body was hurt, but that wasn't what he checked first. That wasn't what was important right then.

He could see his bike lying in the middle of the road. Some spokes looked bent. The seat and handlebars were twisted again. But maybe he could fix it one more time. Just enough to get to the hospital.

That's when he saw it. A huge semi-trailer! A big rig barreling down the road, headed straight for the bike. He waved his arms weakly from the ditch, but it was too late. The driver never saw him. Eighteen wheels flattened his bike. Any hope of Cade riding again that night had been crushed.

Chapter Twenty

Cade held out his hands. Puncture marks crisscrossed his arms like vampire bites. Blood dripped down from his elbows to his palms. He rubbed the gory red smear across his ripped shirt. His legs were just as gruesome. Large patches of skin were missing. His knees were ketchup-red.

He tried standing, but felt faint. Dizzy. He could feel a large, egg-sized lump growing over his right eye. His head must have hit the asphalt when he slammed to the ground. He slumped back down on the pavement to recover. He counted to ten, then took a deep breath and tried again. He was shaky. But he was on his feet. He had to keep going. Just like Mr. Grimsby had said, *You don't quit a race unless they put you in an ambulance.*

The hospital was less than five kilometers away. Straight ahead. He didn't know if he could make it. But he had to try. His dad lay bleeding by the river. His mother and brother were exhausted, getting colder by the minute.

He felt too weak to run. He began to walk with a limp. His legs throbbed with each step. Slowly the ache went away. His legs became dead to the pain. He was able to start hobbling a little faster.

He tried to take his mind off the pain. He thought about Trent having to miss his game the next day. Not being able to play in the biggest battle of the year. He knew how disappointed he would be. How much it meant to him. And to his dad. His father wanted nothing more than to see Trent on the field. Cheer him on from the stands. Watch him throw a touchdown pass. Boast to the other parents that the quarterback was his boy.

Cade wished his dad had wanted to watch *him* at the triathlon. Cheer *him* on. Be proud of *him* when he stood on the podium. If he ever did stand on the podium.

But none of that mattered now. All that mattered was saving his family.

Soon Cade's hobble turned into a jog. He leaned forward and stumbled along as quickly as he could. Drops of blood trailed behind him along the sidewalk. He was too tired to even hold his head up. Every so often he raised his eyes to make sure he was still stumbling in the right direction. Then, from a distance, he spotted the big *H*. The hospital was just a few blocks away. The finish line was dead ahead.

He started to run. Each step hurt more than the one before. His heart pounded like he was at the end of a race.

Nothing could stop him now. He sprinted past the flickering neon sign that said *EMERGENCY*. The doors slid open automatically as he got near. He dashed into the building. He saw a nurse standing down the hall and rushed toward her. But his legs had given all they had to give. He couldn't go one step farther. He collapsed on the tile floor.

"We need a doctor!" the nurse shouted, running to his side.

"Don't worry about me," Cade said.

"You're badly hurt," the nurse said, seeing the blood on his arms and legs.

"But my family's worse."

"What happened?"

"Our car crashed off the bridge into the river," Cade said. "They're still there."

The nurse's eyes widened. "Blindman River?" Cade grimaced as he nodded.

"That's a long way from here."

A doctor rushed down the hall, wheeling a stretcher. "Let's get him on here for treatment," she said.

"We don't just need a stretcher," the nurse said. "We need an ambulance."

"Where was the crash?" the driver asked. He opened the front door of the ambulance ready to climb in.

"The bridge over the Blindman River," Cade said from the stretcher.

"So the other victims are on the bridge?"

"No, they're down by the riverbank. It might be tough to find them."

The driver fixed his eyes on Cade. "Then you're coming with us."

Two paramedics dressed in blue lifted Cade into the back of the ambulance. "You've got some serious wounds," the man said. "We're going to stitch you up as we go. We have to stop the bleeding."

"And you're dehydrated," the woman said, hooking a line from a bag of fluid to his arm.

"Let's roll," the driver said.

A siren pierced the night air. The ambulance sped away from the hospital.

A second emergency vehicle followed close behind.

Cade lay in the back of the ambulance as it raced toward the bridge. The siren wailed as the paramedics continued to bandage his wounds. He hurt all over.

"This will help with the pain," the woman said, handing him a small cup of water and two white pills. Cade blinked his thanks.

He was weak. He was tired. All he wanted to do was sleep. But Cade needed to know his family was okay. *They have to be okay.* It was his last thought before passing out.

Chapter Twenty-One

Cade opened one eye. Just a slit. Just enough to check his wounds. The gashes on his arms were stitched together like Frankenstein. The scrapes on his legs were wrapped in white bandages like The Mummy. He was like a poster boy for a horror-movie double feature.

He opened his second eye. Day had replaced night. Sunlight shone through a window. He glanced around. He wasn't in the ambulance anymore. He was in a hospital room. And he wasn't alone! His mom, dad and Trent were in beds beside and across from him. His grandma and grandpa had just arrived and were about to sit down.

"We thought you'd never wake up," his mom said.

"But you're no Sleeping Beauty," Trent joked. "You look pretty beat up."

"I had a small accident," Cade said, managing a feeble smile.

His mom nodded. "The nurse said you were in bad shape when they found you."

"I didn't know if you guys were going to make it," Cade said. "You weren't doing so well when I left you near the bridge."

"We knew we were going to make it," his mom said.

"What made you so sure?"

"Because we knew *you* were going to make it," his dad said.

Cade's mom leaned forward in her bed. "The paramedics brought us here in the ambulance..."

"But you were the one that saved us," his dad said, holding his arm in a sling.

"They never would have found us without you."

There was a knock on the hospital door. A doctor with a black stethoscope around her neck walked briskly into the room. "Everyone looks like they're doing a lot better this morning," she said, checking her clipboard. "We wanted to monitor you overnight to make sure you were all recovering. That your arm was healing," she said to his dad, "and that you had warmed up from the cold river," she said, giving a nod to Trent and his mom. "You were all close to getting hypothermia."

"So they can go home now?" Grandpa asked from the chair.

"Yes," the doctor said, stopping at the door on her way out. "Everyone is free to go."

"So what are you waiting for?" Grandpa asked.

"What's the rush?" Cade's dad asked.

"I'll tell you what the rush is," his grandpa said, walking over to Trent's bed.

"If we hurry, we can still make it to the big game. We can still watch Trent play."

Cade wished he could close his ears. *Here they go, talking about Trent's football again. And Dad will probably agree with Grandpa. Probably tell Trent he should still play, even after everything that's happened.*

Cade's dad got out of his bed and looked his own father in the eye. "You have got to be kidding."

"No, I never kid about football," Cade's grandpa said. "There's still time for Trent to put on his uniform. Still time for him to make me proud. The pride you never gave me."

"Trent doesn't have to play football to make you or anyone else proud," Cade's dad said. "After last night, we all learned that football's not the most important thing."

Cade glanced at his mom. She was staring at his dad. Her eyes were glistening. She looked proud that he was finally standing up to his father. Cade caught her eye. She gave him a nod.

But what he said next completely shocked Cade.

"And Cade doesn't have to win a triathlon to make us proud either," his dad said, still standing face-to-face with his grandpa. "I don't care if he ever gets on the podium. Just competing is enough. And from now on we're going to watch every triathlon he competes in, believe me."

"Who cares about triathlon?" his grandpa sneered. "It's not a real sport like football."

"No, you're right. It's not like football," Cade's dad said, standing up a bit straighter. "It's a lot tougher."

"Do you seriously believe that?" Grandpa said, throwing up his hands.

"Does football help you escape from a car on the bottom of a river?" his dad asked. "Does football teach you how to rescue your injured parents and get them safely to shore? To swim downstream and find your brother hanging on to a tree for dear life? Does football train you to bike and run twenty kilometers with blood streaming down your arms and legs to get help from a hospital?"

His grandpa's shoulders slumped, and he shook his head in disbelief. "I had no idea. I thought it was just a little fender bender. And no. No, football doesn't do any of that."

Cade looked over at his dad, and they shared a smile. For the first time, his dad was standing where Cade had always wanted him to be. On his side.

Chapter Twenty-Two

Cade sliced through the water. The chlorine burned the cuts on his arms with each stroke. The scabs on his knees stung with every kick. But he was glad to be back in the pool swimming with Mr. Grimsby again. The doctor had said to take a few days off to recover. That his body had been through a lot of stress. He was tired of staying at home though. Tired of sitting on the couch, watching reruns of *The Big Bang Theory*. Of being bored.

Neither he nor Mr. Grimsby had been able to compete in the Alberta Triathlon the week before. They'd had bigger things to worry about that day. Cade had told him about the car crash and rescue. And Mr. Grimsby had described his painful day at his wife's funeral. They both wanted to put those memories behind them. Move on. Entering another race was just the way to do it. The Edmonton Triathlon was coming up the following month. Cade's mom and dad had said he could go. And they'd promised to drive him. In the new car bought to replace the old one, still sitting on the bottom of the Blindman River.

There was a lot of hard work to do before the race. He and Mr. Grimsby had to keep training. Swimming in the pool was a lot easier than swimming in a lake like he'd have to do in Edmonton. He didn't have to worry about waves hitting him smack in the face. Or watch out for the big yellow buoy floating out in the middle of the lake. It was a lot easier than rescuing someone from a cold river too. He only had to worry about the laps he and Mr. Grimsby were swimming. One hundred lengths of the pool before they went to Subway to wolf down a couple of foot-long subs. It had become their tradition after a tough workout.

Cade's arms windmilled. His legs kicked easily behind him. Despite his bumps, bruises and scrapes, he seemed faster than ever. *All the swimming, biking and running during the rescue must have made me stronger*. It was as if he'd actually done the Sylvan Lake triathlon—but at top speed. Quicker than he ever could have done the real race. He was in a lot better shape now than when he had been just a swimmer. He wondered how he would do if he was still on the swim team.

One last stroke, and Cade glided to the wall.

"Well, look who it is!"

He lifted his head out of the water and saw Gavin staring down at him.

"It's Cade the Blade—skinny as a blade of grass."

Gavin was still in his suit though the Blue Sharks had already finished their early-morning training.

"Aren't you the guy who wasn't good enough for our swim team?" Gavin said in a mocking voice.

"Yeah, that's me," Cade said, in as friendly a way as he could. He didn't want to start an argument.

"The guy who comes here twice a week with that old man?"

"Mr. Grimsby is a friend of mine."

"Well, neither one of you looks very good. I can see why Coach kicked you off the team."

Cade gritted his teeth. "You know he didn't kick me off the team. I left to do something else."

"Maybe you did," Gavin scoffed, "but it sure wasn't to become a better swimmer."

Cade pulled himself out of the water and stood squarely in front of the Blue Shark, who stood tall and puffed out his chest. "You think you're so good, Gavin?"

"Yeah, I do. Best freestyler on the team. Got a bronze at the Summer Games."

"Then prove it."

"What are you talking about?"

"You heard me," Cade said, putting his hands on his hips. "Let's go, right now. Two laps. The winner gets to say they're the best swimmer."

"And I'll be the judge," a girl said.

Cade and Gavin both turned to see Jazz marching up to them. "If you guys want to race, go ahead. I'll stand at the wall and see who touches first."

"You mean, me touching the wall first," Gavin said.

"We'll just have to wait and see," Jazz said, giving Cade a sly smile.

Jazz and Mr. Grimsby stood at the edge of the pool. Cade and Gavin crouched beside them, ready to start. Jazz raised her arm. Then dropped it fast.

"Go!"

The two boys launched themselves into the pool. They dove deep like dolphins, then surfaced farther down their lanes. Their arms thrashed the water as they matched each other stroke for stroke. Their feet kicked up wakes of white froth. There was no difference between them. They were tied at the first turn.

Cade flip-turned and pushed off the wall. Just one length to go. He turned his head to take a breath and could see Gavin inching ahead. But he didn't panic. He relaxed his breathing just like Mr. Grimsby had taught him to do. Then he found a higher gear. A speed that came from all the training he and Mr. Grimsby had done. From all the extra biking and running. The biking and running he knew Gavin had never done.

He exploded forward. He knew the finish was coming. He could see the wall dead ahead. He put his head down. He wouldn't breathe for the last four strokes. He pulled his arms and kicked his legs with everything he had left.

Then he touched.

He wondered if it had been enough. If he had been strong enough, fast enough, focused enough right to the finish line. Win or lose, he knew he had done his best. And that was all that mattered.

"Cade is the winner!" Jazz shouted above him.

He held on to the side of the pool. His chest heaved. His mouth gasped for air. He almost couldn't believe it. He had beaten the fastest swimmer on the Blue Sharks.

"I knew you could do it!" Mr. Grimsby cheered, punching the air with his fist.

"Me too," Jazz said, bending down to give him a high five.

Cade reached across the floating lane divider to shake Gavin's hand. But Gavin was having none of it. He pulled himself out of the water. Then he grabbed a towel and slinked off to the change room.

"Gavin doesn't look very happy," Cade said, still breathing hard.

Jazz nodded. "Not right now, but he'll be back. A little competition will just make him work harder."

Mr. Grimsby and Jazz weren't the only ones who had watched the race. Coach Pedersen had been keeping an eye on the grudge match. He walked over from his small office. "Congratulations, Cade, that was quite a finish."

"Thanks, Coach."

"You're better than I remember. How would you like to swim with the Blue Sharks again?"

"Thanks," Cade said. "But I think I'll stick with triathlon for now."

Coach frowned at first, then smiled and raised an eyebrow. "With a little more work, I think you could be on the podium."

"Some things are more important than standing on the podium."

"What could be more important than getting a medal?" Coach asked.

Cade shot a smile at Mr. Grimsby and Jazz.

"Friends."

Eric Howling is the author of six other sports novels: *Gang Tackle, Head Hunter, Red Zone Rivals, Hoop Magic, Kayak Combat* and *Drive*. His books have been shortlisted for the Hackmatack Children's Choice Book Award, included on *Resource Links'* Year's Best list and picked as CCBC Best Books selections. Eric lives and plays sports in Calgary, Alberta. Learn more at www.erichowling.wordpress.com.

Titles in the Series

orca sports

orca sports

For more information on all the books in the Orca Sports series, please visit **www.orcabook.com**.